hannah and jack

by Mary Nethery
Illustrations by Mary Morgan

Atheneum Books for Young Readers

Atheneum Books for Young Readers
An imprint of Simon & Schuster Children's Publishing Division
1230 Avenue of the Americas
New York, New York 10020

The text of this book is set in 16 pt. Cochin.
The illustrations are rendered in watercolor and gouache.

Printed in Hong Kong
First edition

10 9 8 7 6 5 4 3 2 1

LIBRARY OF CONGRESS CATALOGING-IN-
PUBLICATION DATA
Nethery, Mary.
Hannah and Jack/by Mary Nethery; illustrated by Mary Morgan. — 1st ed.
p. cm.
Summary: While vacationing with Grandma, Hannah finds a way to stay in touch with her
best friend, Jack, the cat.
ISBN 0-689-80533-0
[I. Cats — Fiction. 2. Vacations — Fiction. 3. Grandmothers — Fiction.]
1. Morgan, Mary, date- ill. II. Title.
PZ7.N4388Han 1996
93-4651
[E] — dc20

To Han, H.A., and Jackie . . . my three golden loves
—M. N.

For my friends Anita, Kato, Kathy, Shaun, and Terri
—M. M.

Hannah loved her cat.

His eyes were big as copper pennies, and Hannah liked the way his tail spiked up, then jiggedy-jigged at the tip. His fur smelled like warm gingerbread. His nose whistled when he purred.

Wherever Hannah went, Jack was sure to go. Hannah
hunted fairies. Jack hunted garden snakes.

Hannah threw his toy. Jack chased it back.

Hannah built a castle. Jack stormed it down.

Every night Hannah told Jack a bedtime story. Then Hannah ate a treat, and Jack cleaned up the crumbs.

One day Hannah's mother and father packed for a trip.

"We're going to Grandma's house!" shouted Hannah.

She thought Jack looked pleased.

Hannah packed for two. A suitcase for her, and one for Jack.

They were ready.

But Hannah's father unpacked Jack.
"You can't take Jack with you, Hannah," he said.

Hannah held Jack to her.

"Who will tell Jack his bedtime stories?" she cried. "Who will tell him how pretty he is?"

"The trip is too long for Jack," her father said.

"Mrs. Gurney will take good care of him," said her mother.

Hannah squeezed Jack.

"Don't cry, Jack," she whispered in his ear. "I will think about you all the time."

Then she gave him a long kiss good-bye.

Hannah thought about Jack every day of the trip.

"Look at the beautiful forest, Hannah," said her father.

"Lots of snakes in there," said Hannah. "Jack likes snakes."

"Smell the clean ocean air," said her mother.

"Smells like fish," said Hannah. "Jack likes fish."

"Listen to the birds in the mountains," said her father.

"Jack likes birds," said Hannah.

Her mother looked at her.

"Grandma has a new dog," she said. "You can play with him."

When they got to Grandma's house, Grandma showed Hannah her new dog. That night he came to see Hannah. But he didn't like bedtime stories. And he was very greedy about donuts.

Grandma's dog left when the lights went out.

I'm thinking about you, Jack, Hannah thought. Don't be afraid of the dark.

"Would you like to take Grandma's dog for a walk?" asked her father the next morning.

"He's not much fun," said Hannah.

"No time for walks," said Grandma. "Hannah and I are going out."

So Hannah and Grandma
went to the circus. Hannah ate
cotton candy and clapped for
the Trapeezi Brothers, but all
the big cats reminded her of
Jack. I hope Mrs. Gurney
kisses Jack good night,
she thought.

"Would you like a nice postcard to remember the acrobats?" asked Grandma.

"No, thank you," said Hannah.

"You have so few smiles today, Hannah dear," said Grandma. "Is something troubling you?"

Hannah closed her eyes. She tried to smell Jack's ginger fur and hear his whistle purr. But she couldn't.

"I miss Jack."

"I'm sure Jack misses you, too," Grandma said. "What shall we do?"

Hannah thought. Jack might fly to Grandma's in an airplane. Or he might catch a taxi. But he couldn't do those things by himself.

Suddenly, she remembered what her mother always did when she went on a trip and Hannah had to stay at home.

"I know what to do!" shouted Hannah.

She chose a shiny postcard of a tiger. She told Grandma what to write on the back. Then she mailed it to Jack.

That week Hannah and Grandma did many things together. They rode a train around the zoo. They saw elephants and zebras, giraffes and birds. Hannah sent Jack a postcard of an ostrich.

"May I buy a
rubber snake?" asked Hannah.

"That will make a lovely souvenir," said
Grandma. She paid the woman in the gift shop.

They splished and splashed at the beach. Hannah collected a
jar of sand and shells. She mailed Jack a postcard with a
picture of a real fish on it.

They went to the Bengal Room for tea. They ordered raspberries and cream, cakes and jam.

"Please put this cupcake in a doggy bag," Hannah said to the waiter.

She sent Jack a postcard of people eating desserts.

Dear Hannah,
Thank you for the postcards. Not to worry. Mrs. Gurney is a lovely woman. She takes special care of me. See you soon.

Jack

Not long before Hannah and her parents were to leave for home, an envelope arrived at Grandma's with Hannah's name on it. Something fell out. A picture of Jack!

Well, the handwriting didn't look a thing like Jack's. But the letter *was* signed with his pawprint.

The moment Hannah got home, she squeezed Jack until he coughed.

"Let's have a party!" she shouted. "A Glad-to-Be-Back Party!"

They romped around in the sea sand. They opened Jack's present. Then Hannah put the cupcake on Jack's plate.

"No crumbs for you today," she said.

After the party, they lolled like fat rabbits in the sweet grass, just being together again.